This

Matzah Ball Book

belongs to:

_____

_____

_____

Klutzy   Shmutzy

Kvetchy   Shluffy   Noshy

Klutzy Boy

by Anne-Marie Baila Asner

MATZAH BALL BOOKS®

Klutzy Boy is the clumsiest kid on the block.

If there's something to spill . . .

"Oh, no! I'm all wet."

Something to break . . .

"Oops! I didn't mean to hit the window."

Or an injury to be had . . .

"Ow! My leg hurts."

Just leave it to Klutzy Boy.

Every day, Klutzy Boy walks home from school with Shleppy Boy. Shleppy Boy always has a lot to carry, but one day he had even more than usual, since it had been his turn for show-and-tell.

"Klutzy Boy, would you mind carrying my fish bowl?" asked Shleppy Boy. "I just have too much to carry. I can't shlepp it all."

"Of course," said Klutzy Boy, who was happy to help.

Shleppy Boy handed Klutzy Boy the bowl and said, "Be sure to be careful!"

As soon as the words left Shleppy Boy's mouth,
the fish bowl hit the ground with a smash.

"Oh, no!" said Klutzy Boy. "It slipped right out of my
hands! I didn't mean to . . . ."

"Klutzy Boy!" said Shleppy Boy angrily. "You are so, so, so . . . . klutzy!"

Upset, Shleppy Boy left Klutzy Boy to deal with the mess and to walk home alone.

The next day at school, Klutzy Boy's other friends could tell something was the matter.

Kvetchy Boy, who never misses an opportunity to complain, advised, "Maybe if you complain about your problem, you might feel better."

But Klutzy Boy was in no mood to kvetch. It wouldn't help him be less clumsy.

Noshy Boy, who loves to eat, said, "Maybe you need a snack. Do you want one of my cookies?"

But Klutzy Boy knew that noshing wouldn't make him less klutzy.

Shluffy Girl, who is always sleepy, suggested, "Maybe you need a nap. It always makes me feel better."

Klutzy Boy just shook his head. He knew that shluffing wouldn't cure his clumsiness.

"Well, Klutzy Boy," said Shluffy Girl. "If whatever is bothering you can't be fixed with a shluff, a nosh or a kvetch, what could possibly be the problem?"

"Shluffy Girl," answered Klutzy Boy. "I am the klutziest kid in the whole wide world. I even dropped Shleppy Boy's fish bowl!"

"That's it? That's why you're so upset?" asked Shluffy Girl between yawns.

"Uh, yes," said Klutzy Boy, looking confused.

"Klutzy Boy, all you have to do is pay a little more attention to what you're doing and take your time," said Shluffy Girl. "You'll see you'll be a lot less clumsy."

At first, Klutzy Boy didn't believe that being less
klutzy could be that easy. But he gave it a try, and
soon Klutzy Boy spilled a lot less, broke fewer things
and got hurt less often. A little extra time and
attention left Klutzy Boy a lot less klutzy.

Klutzy Boy even brought Shleppy Boy a new fish
bowl without dropping it.

Sometimes when Klutzy Boy is excited or in a hurry or forgets to pay attention to what he is doing . . .

"Oops!"

Klutzy Boy is reminded that he still can be a little klutzy. Just like most everyone else.

Kvetchy   Shluffy   Noshy

Klutzy   Shmutzy

Glossary
A Bissle (little bit) of Yiddish

Bubbe (bŭ-bē) *n.* grandmother

Keppy (kĕpp-ē) *n.* head; *adj.* smart, using one's head

Kibbitzy (kĭbbĭtz-ē) *v. kibbitz* to joke around; *adj. kibbitzy*

Klutzy (klŭts-ē) *adj.* clumsy

Kvelly (k'vĕll-ē) *v. kvell* to be proud, pleased; *adj. kvelly*

Kvetchy (k'vĕtch-ē) *adj.* whiny, complaining

Noshy (nŏsh-ē) *v. nosh* to snack; *adj. noshy*

Shayna Punim (shā-nă pŭ-nĭm) *adj.* pretty *(shayna)*; *n.* face *(punim)*

Shleppy (shlĕp-ē) *v. shlep* to carry or drag; *adj. shleppy*

Shluffy (shlŭf-ē) *adj.* sleepy, tired

Shmoozy (shmooz-ē) *adj.* chatty, friendly

Shmutzy (shmŭtz-ē) *adj.* dirty, messy

Tushy (tŭsh-ē) *n.* buttocks, bottom

Zaide (zā-dē) *n.* grandfather

For information about Matzah Ball Books, visit

www.matzahballbooks.com

MATZAH BALL BOOKS®

 **MATZAH BALL BOOKS®**

Products

◀ **toddler tee**
sizes: 2T & 4T

youth & adult tees ▶
sizes: S, M, L

◀ **infant set**

Noshy Boy dish set ▶

Shmutzy Girl dish set ▶

HOW TO ORDER:

• website: www.matzahballbooks.com
• e-mail: orders@matzahballbooks.com
• phone: (310) 936-5683

3JED000008478X